JOURNEY TO FREEDOM

A Story of the Underground Railroad

Courtni C. Wright
illustrated by Gershom Griffith

Holiday House/New York

To my sister Joni, my niece Ria, and my nephew Rob
—C.C.W.

To Sallie—my heart will always ring
to the sound of your laughter
—G.G.

Library of Congress Cataloging-in-Publication Data
Wright, Courtni Crump.
Journey to Freedom: A Story of the Underground Railroad
Courtni C. Wright; illustrated by Gershom
Griffith.—1st ed.
p.   cm.
Summary: Joshua and his family, runaway slaves from a tobacco
plantation in Kentucky, follow the Underground Railroad to freedom.
ISBN 0-8234-1096-X
[1. Underground railroad—Fiction.   2. Slavery—Fiction.   3. Afro-
Americans—Fiction.]   I. Griffith, Gershom, ill.   II. Title.
PZ7.W9348Rai   1994   93-41745   CIP   AC
[E]—dc20

The early November nights in the forest are very dark, silent, and cold. There is only the hooting of owls to keep us company. Mama speaks softly into my ear, "Be quiet, Joshua! You got to whisper." It is hard to be quiet all the time when you are only eight years old, but I try to obey. My ten-year-old brother, Nathan, and I want so much to sing or play hide-and-seek. Papa says there will be plenty of time for that when our journey is over.

We are runaway slaves from a tobacco plantation near Lexington, Kentucky. We are traveling on the Underground Railroad with eight others. Harriet Tubman is the conductor and is leading us to freedom in the North. She used to be a slave in Maryland but ran away to Pennsylvania. Now she helps other slaves.

Miss Tubman makes us travel quickly. She wants to get all of us to the North before newspaper articles appear about our escape. Just a few weeks ago, Master Grant read us an article about runaway slaves from a neighboring plantation. He warned us not to try it.

WANTED!!!
RUNAWAY SLAVES FROM LIVE OAK PLANTATION
Reward $500 for the male $350 each for the woman and children!!

We travel through the dense forest at night so that patrollers won't catch us. They would take us back to the plantation, and Master Grant would beat us for sure.

Papa is not afraid of being beaten. Master has taken the whip to him many times. Papa worries more that he would sell us apart. Many slave families do not live together. My family does because Mama is the favorite cook on the plantation, and Papa is Master's best horse handler. Whenever Master wanted to scare Mama and Papa, he would threaten to sell Nathan and me "down the river" to the Deep South.

"Stop! Listen! Do you hear it?" Miss Tubman strains to see through the darkness of the forest. The fog is so dense, we cannot see past the trees in front of us.

We look in the direction Miss Tubman is pointing, but we see nothing. Then, from far away, we hear the barking of dogs. The sound gets louder and louder as they come closer and closer. Patrollers could be right behind them.

Quickly, we rush into the heavy underbrush. Papa shelters us with his body as the other men and Miss Tubman crouch nearby. I can feel the tension in the bodies of the men.

"Who is it, Papa? Can they see us?" I whisper.

Papa motions for me to keep quiet. He pushes Nathan deeper into the vines beside Mama. She wraps her arms around me, holding me close to her chest. Her heart flutters against my back like a frightened bird.

A pack of six snarling dogs appears through the fog. Their ears lie flat against their heads. Water smelling of decaying leaves drips from their matted, dirty fur. They stop only feet from our hiding place. Frothy saliva covers their mouths. Their breath makes puffs of smoke in the cold night air. I can hear them panting as they sniff, trying to find us.

Miss Tubman whispers into Papa's ear, "I don't hear no horses or men. They just a pack of wild dogs looking for somethin' to eat. They smell the meat and follow us. Throw your food to 'em. Maybe they go away."

Papa and the men throw the last of our food into the undergrowth behind the dogs. The animals growl and snarl as they devour the biscuits and meat. For the moment, they have forgotten about us. Licking their whiskers, the dogs sniff the ground, looking for more.

The leader of the pack slowly creeps toward our hiding place. He crawls on his belly. The end of his tail flicks from side to side. Mama tightens her arm around me and reaches for Nathan.

Papa looks at the other men. They nod in agreement. I can feel their bodies tighten. Suddenly they spring up, waving their arms in the air and shouting, "Yah! Yah!"

The dogs freeze in their tracks. Their leader stops, too. Their breath makes tiny vapor clouds as they crouch close to the ground. Then they turn and run into the foggy night, whimpering in fear. In moments, the forest is quiet again.

Miss Tubman steps into the clearing looking after the dogs. In a low, husky voice she sings, "Steal away. Steal away to Jesus." The song is her signal that it is safe for us to come out. As Mama, Nathan, and I crawl from the vines, she says, "All right, everybody, let's start walkin'. We can't stay here. Someone might'a heard the shoutin' and the dogs."

We have been passengers on the Underground Railroad for almost twenty days and are nearing the end of our journey. As we start walking again, Papa looks back over his shoulder. He sees and hears nothing. He picks up our parcel of clothes and puts one arm around my shoulders. Mama takes Nathan's hand. We hurry to catch up with Miss Tubman.

Papa says we are lucky to have Miss Tubman as our conductor on the Railroad. She has led so many people out of the South to freedom in the North that everyone calls her Moses. She is like the Moses of the Bible who led the Jews out of bondage under the pharaoh.

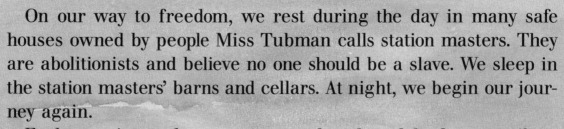

On our way to freedom, we rest during the day in many safe houses owned by people Miss Tubman calls station masters. They are abolitionists and believe no one should be a slave. We sleep in the station masters' barns and cellars. At night, we begin our journey again.

Each morning at dawn, we stop at the edge of the forest until we see the station master hang a quilt on the porch railing. If it has the color black in its pattern, we walk into the yard. It is the "All's clear" sign known only by the conductors and station masters on the Railroad.

This morning Miss Tubman sees the quilt and motions us to the barn. Once inside, the station master, Mr. Anderson, closes the door and lights a lantern. We follow him up the ladder to the hayloft. Bales of hay hide a door to a small room. It has no windows but smells sweet from the straw-stuffed sleeping pallets. Straw also covers the floor to muffle the sound of our footsteps. We will spend the day in this room.

Mrs. Anderson brings us some hot stew and biscuits and also some blankets. The food tastes good after a night in the cold forest.

Before going to sleep, I whisper in Papa's ear, "How much longer 'fore we be free?"

Papa thinks for a minute and then replies, "We got maybe three more days to walk 'fore we reach Canada. Then we be free and safe. Now go to sleep."

   In the stuffy air of the secret room, I listen to the snoring of the
other passengers on the train. Some of them have left their families
behind on plantations. They plan to send for them when they save
enough money from their wages as free men. Others were sold
away from their families and decided to run away rather than live
on the new plantations.

   The journey has not been easy on any of us. Mama hurt her ankle
on the third day. Papa and Nathan had to carry her in a seat they
made with their arms and hands. She still walks with a limp, and
her ankle swells up from the fifteen miles we travel every night.
Mama tried to persuade Papa to leave us on the plantation, but he
would not listen. I heard him say that nothing would separate him
from us. Nothing.

"Wake up, everybody. Time to go." It's dusk, and Miss Tubman's voice fills the silence of the room.

The air is very cold as we step out of the barn into the darkness. We pull our thin clothing tightly around our bodies as we begin the night's walk. I overhear Miss Tubman whisper to the station master as we leave, "I hopes the snow holds off 'til we reach Canada. Their clothes is threadbare. They ain't of no use in very cold weather. Most of 'em ain't even got shoes."

I look down at my own bare feet and wiggle my toes in the crispy grass. Snow! I heard about it in the books Mistress Elizabeth reads out loud to her children, but I have never seen it. At Christmas, Mistress put out something she called a "snowmobile." I sneaked into the parlor one time and shook it when no one was looking. Thick flakes of white covered the little house inside the glass dome. I don't say anything to Miss Tubman, but I hope it will snow.

A cold wind begins to blow after we have been walking about three hours. No stars twinkle in the night. Papa puts his arm around my shoulders to warm me up. Mama hugs Nathan close. We shiver in our thin clothes.

Suddenly strange white flakes float down from the sky. I know at once that this is snow. At first only a few flakes dance in the wind. I catch one and hold it on the palm of my hand for a second. It is shaped like the tatted lace collar on Mistress's red velvet dress. It leaves a small, wet spot on my hand when it melts. With each step we take, more and more flakes fill the air. They stick to my eyelashes and melt on my tongue.

In the darkness, I hear Nathan whisper, "My feet's numb. I can't feel my toes, Papa. Help me!"

Miss Tubman stops. "Use your hands to warm 'em," she whispers to Papa. "Hold the boy's feet 'til the toes start tinglin'. Then tear off pieces of this blanket to wrap 'em in. It's the best we can do. I pray he don't get frostbit."

Papa follows her instructions in the darkness. Nathan says he feels better, but Papa has to help him walk. Nathan makes a muffled, grunting sound with each step.

Soon the snow is too deep for us to travel through. Thick flakes cover my hair and shoulders. I brush them off and wrap myself in a blanket Miss Tubman gives me. She has carried them tied to her back with a rope that crosses over her chest since we left the last safe house.

"We gotta stop here. We can't travel no more tonight," she says to the men as she hands blankets to them, too. "Help me make a shelter under these vines."

Miss Tubman and the men push aside the deep growth of the forest until they open a space large enough for all of us. Then they cover the vines with two of the blankets. The driving snow quickly sticks, turning them white. We crawl inside. The closeness of our bodies heats our shelter.

Soon, we get sleepy in our tent. Papa says no one will find us under this thick layer of vines, twigs, blankets, and snow. We are safe from animals, too. Nathan whispers, "My feet's better now, Papa. See, I can wiggle my toes again."

In the morning, Miss Tubman eases open a small space in the tent. "Miss Tubman," Ma whispers, "where you goin'?"

"To look around. I hopes we can make up the distance we lost last night 'cause of the storm," she says. Bright sunlight streams through the bare tree branches.

She does not stay long. When she comes back inside, the corners of her mouth are turned down and wrinkles line her forehead. She shakes her head and says, "The sun's too bright. Patrollers lookin' for us see our footprints for sure. We'll have to spend the day here. I hopes the station master won't worry too much. There's no way for him to know we be late."

I snuggle closer to Mama and whisper, "Mama, I's so hungry. You think Papa find somethin' for me to eat?"

Without answering, Mama reaches into the pocket of her tattered apron and pulls out a biscuit she saved from our supper at the last safe house. I know she is hungry, too, but she divides it between Nathan and me.

Night comes slowly. The cold chills our bones as we leave the hiding place. The walking is hard in the waist-deep snow, but finally we reach the station. The station master, Mr. Nelson, is very happy to see us. Before he closes the root-cellar door, he says to Miss Tubman, "Tomorrow night, you'll reach Sandusky, Ohio. From there you'll cross Lake Erie by boat into Ontario, Canada."

Boat! I've never been on a boat! Mama's eyes grow large with worry when she hears this, but Papa gently pats her hand.

"Why can't we stay here, Mr. Nelson?" Nathan asks. "We a long way from Kentucky. Nobody lookin' for us."

"It's not safe to stay here," he explains. "The Fugitive Slave Act

says that any runaway slave found in another state will be arrested and sent back to the South."

Pa says hoarsely, "We come so far. I won't be turned back now."

The last night of walking seems to last forever. The air is colder, but it does not snow again. All the little creeks and streams along the way have frozen. Icicles cling to the low-hanging branches and sparkle like the prisms on Mistress's crystal chandelier. They crack off and fall into the snow as we trudge past. I break off one and suck on it. It quickly melts in my mouth. The cold water slides down my throat. I look at Papa and exclaim softly, "Papa, there's icicles in your new mustache!" He chuckles as he brushes them off.

A rowboat waits for us on the shore. Captain Miller waves to us as we walk from the forest. He hugs Miss Tubman and helps her aboard first. I'm second. As we shove off, Mama whispers, "Dear Lord, please protect my family on this last leg of our journey. Guide our captain to safety on the shore. Amen."

The water on the lake is smooth and calm. A lantern on the bow of the boat lights our way. It shines off the water like candles in a mirror. Captain Miller says we're lucky tonight. Lake Erie can be very rough and choppy. Mama says her prayers have been answered. Papa holds us close as the spray from the lake blows wet and cold in our faces.

On the other side, Miss Tubman thanks Captain Miller for our safe trip. We are in Canada, and we are free! Papa is so happy that he runs and prances like a young deer. He hugs Mama and swings her around and around. Mama is laughing and crying so hard that she cannot tell him to stop. Nathan takes me by the hands, and we dance around in circles, too. Someone twirls Miss Tubman in the air, until she cries out "Stop!"

When the first joy and excitement of freedom are over, Miss Tubman leads us in a prayer of thanksgiving to God. We all bow our heads as she says, "Heavenly Father, we thanks you for our safe journey out of slavery and for all the good, kind folks who fed us and gave us shelter on our way. Amen."

Tom, one of the men who traveled with us, adds a prayer for Miss Tubman. "Lord, bless this gentle, brave woman. Give her the strength to carry on in your name."

Everyone says a loud "Amen."

Miss Tubman leads us to a church where we eat our first food as free people. It is a simple meal of vegetable beef stew and cornbread muffins, but it's the best I've ever tasted. Tears sparkle on Mama's cheeks, and Papa says over and over, "Free at last."

AUTHOR'S NOTE

In the mid-1800s, the Underground Railroad was a network of "safe houses" in which enslaved African-Americans called "passengers" slept and ate in barns, cellars, and secret rooms during the day. At night, the passengers continued their northward journey, often on foot, as they escaped to freedom in Canada. The term "underground" was used because the help was given in secret; the "station masters" who hid the runaways were breaking the Fugitive Slave Law passed in 1850. It stated that Underground Railroad workers could be fined $1,000.00 or be put in prison for six months if they were discovered helping an enslaved person escape. Once caught, runaways had to be returned to their owners in the South. The station masters also were called "abolitionists" because they believed that slavery was unjust and should be ended. The term "conductor" was used to describe a person like Harriet Tubman, who led runaways to freedom.

—C.C.W.

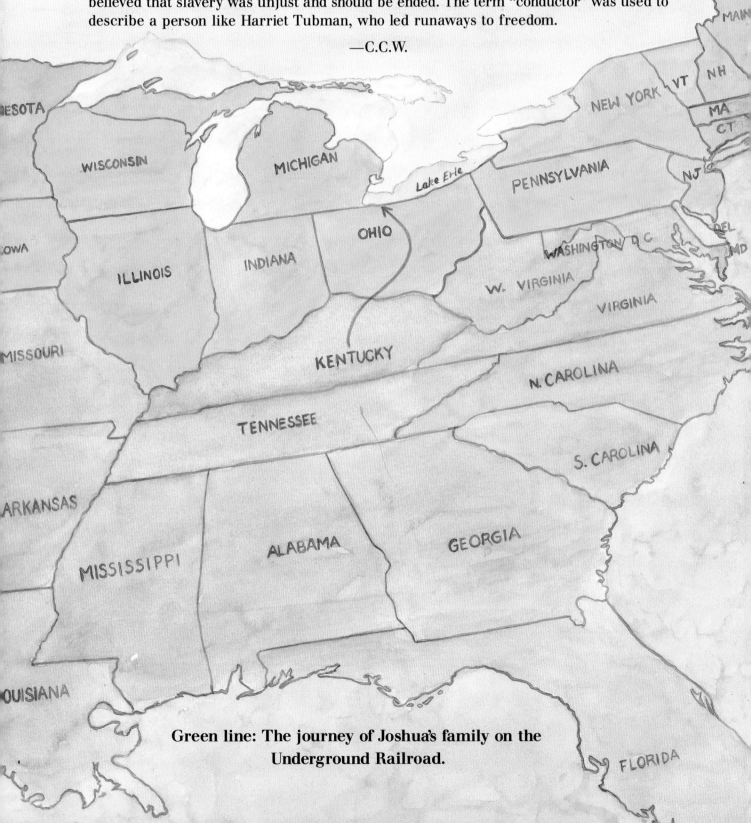

Green line: The journey of Joshua's family on the Underground Railroad.